THE ABC FACTOR

Written by
Katrina Charman
Illustrated by
Tony Neal

Audition to be in a new ABC Book!
No pushing
No biting or growling
No ordinary animals!!!

Farshore

Every day, Stick Insect sat in
a tree, pretending to be a stick.
Or sometimes a twig. It wasn't much fun.

Then, one day, he saw a very
exciting poster . . .

"A starring role in a book!"
gasped Stick Insect.

For Charlie Cooper,

Brick, Piper and Riley – K.C.

For Olive – T. N.

Farshore

First published in Great Britain 2021 by Farshore
An imprint of HarperCollins*Publishers*
1 London Bridge Street, London SE1 9GF
www.farshore.co.uk

HarperCollins*Publishers*
1st Floor, Watermarque Building, Ringsend Road
Dublin 4, Ireland

ISBN 978 1 4052 9857 5
Printed in China.
1

A CIP catalogue record for this title is available from the British Library.

HAVE YOU GOT . . .
THE
ABC
FACTOR
Audition today to be in the most amazing animal alphabet book EVER!

He dashed off to join the queue.

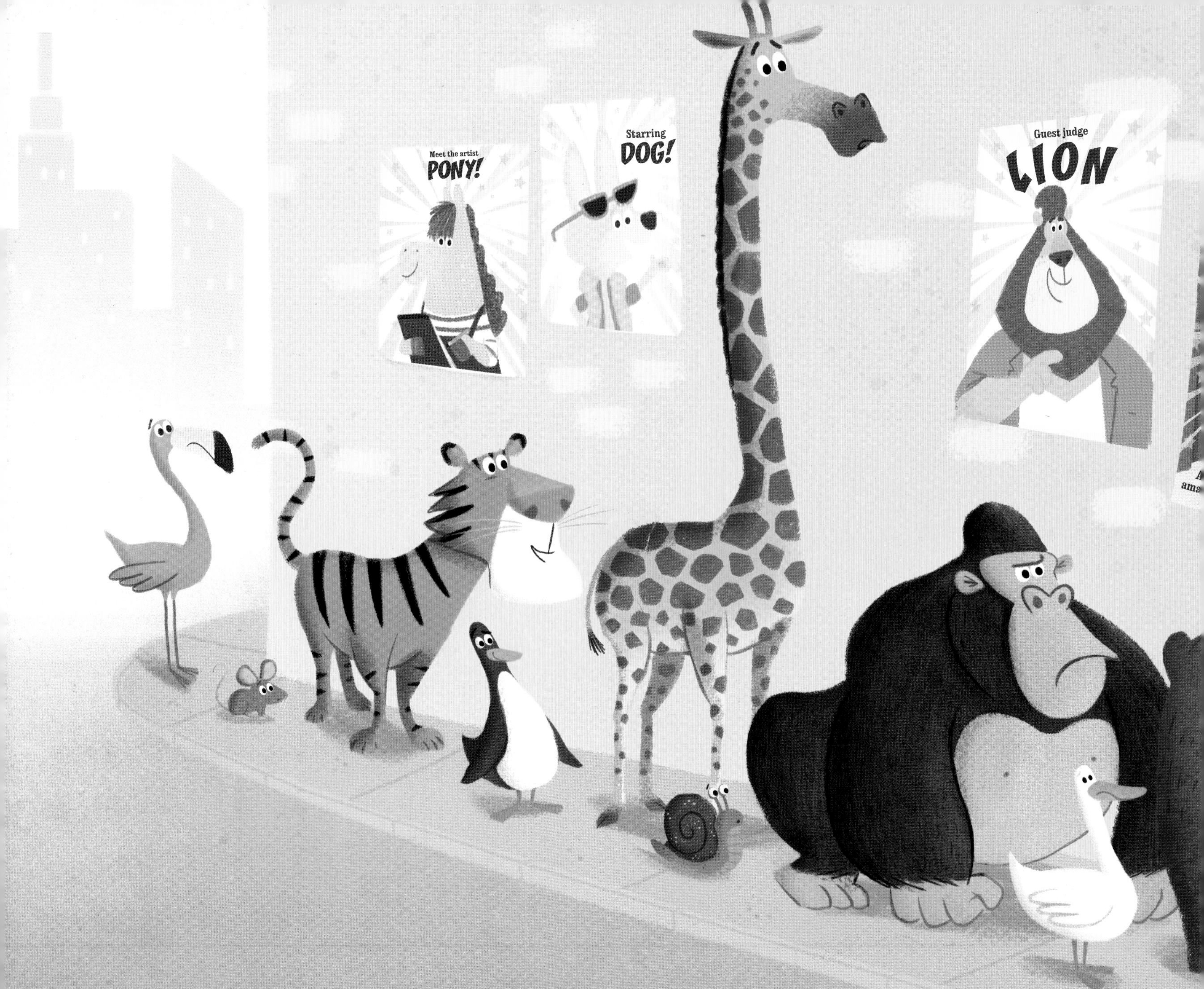

But a very important-looking elephant was turning lots of animals away.

“Ant – no! Bear – no! Cat – no!”

“That’s not fair!” moaned Cat.

“Sorry,” said Elephant. “The author doesn’t want ordinary animals for her ABC. She’s looking for something different.”

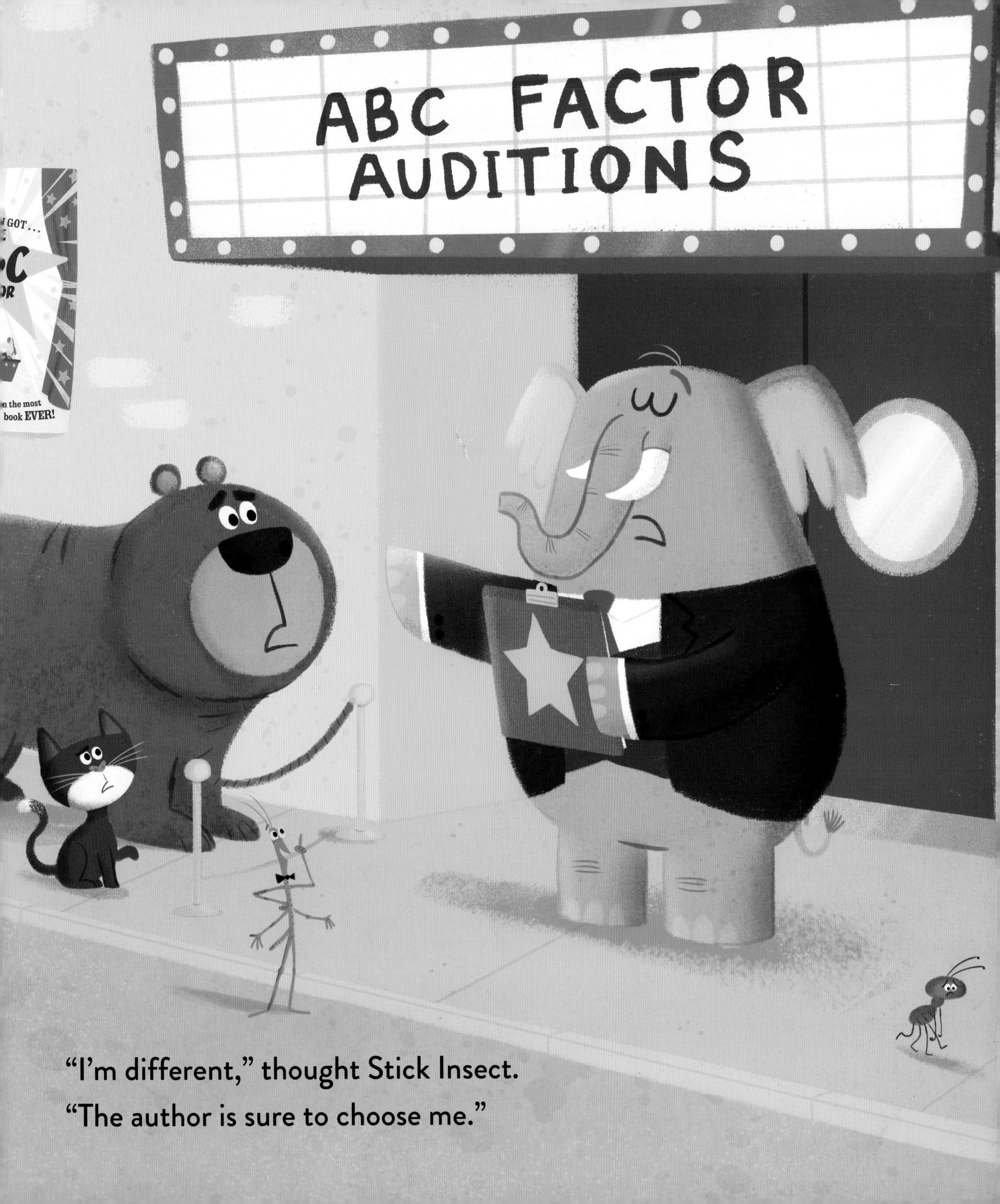

"I'm different," thought Stick Insect.
"The author is sure to choose me."

Inside the theatre, Elephant introduced the ABC Factor judges.

"Give a big hand to our super-special author . . .

Dog!

"Dog has starred in sixteen alphabet books. Now she's creating her very own unique **ABC**!

"Next, our amazing illustrator . . .

Pony!

Pony can draw absolutely anything."

"Except ponies!" said Pony.

"And horses."

"Last but not least,
here's our very special
guest judge . . .

Lion!

"King of the ABCs, Lion has starred in twenty-two alphabet books—"
"Twenty-five!" roared Lion. "And a movie."
Everyone cheered. It was time for the judging to begin.

First came the letter A.

Anaconda, Axolotl and Aye-Aye trooped on to the stage.

The judges whispered together, deciding which was the most unusual. Then Dog announced:

"**A** is for . . . **Axolotl**! Congratulations! You're in our book!"

Next came the Bs.
There was:
Brontosaurus,
Bandicoot
and . . .

"Stick Insect?" frowned Dog.

"B is for Bug," explained Stick Insect.

"Bugs are **boring!**" Lion roared, and Dog announced:

"**B** is for . . . **Brontosaurus!**"

The judges chose:

Capybara for **C**,

Dodo for **D**,

Echidna for **E**,

and **F** went to **Flying Squirrel**.

Then came the letter G.
Gnat, Giant Land Snail and Glow Worm buzzed, crept and wriggled on to the stage.

"Gnat belongs with the Ns!" said Lion.

"No, I don't!" said Gnat. "The 'G' is silent."

The judges agreed that was very unusual indeed.
"**G** is for . . . **Gnat**!" they cried.

Next, Hammerhead Shark, Hyena and Horse lined up on the stage.

“I can’t draw horses!” wailed Pony. “We need a different H.”

Stick Insect had an idea.
"I'm a Herbivore," he said.
"I only eat plants."
The judges weren't impressed.

"**H** is for . . . **H-h-hammerhead Shark!**" stuttered Dog.

Stick Insect was disappointed. But he stayed put for the letter I, alongside Iguana and another very odd-looking animal. "I'm an Ibis," explained the creature. "A type of bird."

"No, you're not!" cried Dog. "You're a CAT! And there are way too many cat books."

Then Lion frowned at Stick Insect.
"Don't tell me: I is for Insect? Too ordinary!"

And Dog announced: "**I** is for . . . **Iguana**!"

Stick Insect returned sadly to his seat, as **J** went to **Jackalope**.

Kangaroo and King Cobra lined up for K.
"No snakes!" yelped Dog. "They're too slithery!"

"But they're really easy to draw," said Pony.

"And I'm a King Cobra!" protested the snake. "I'm royalty."
"Fine," sighed Dog. "**K** is for **King Cobra**!"

The next three letters passed by quickly.

"L is for . . . **Lemmings!**"

"M is for . . . **Manatee!**"

"N is for . . . **Naked Mole Rat!**"

"But you'll have to put some clothes on," added Dog. "This is a children's book."

The judges couldn't agree at all on **O**, **P**, **Q** and **R**.

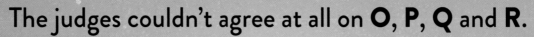

"Perhaps you should decide on those later?" suggested Elephant.

The judges still looked grumpy, but they sat down.

S was next. Stick Insect was excited now. S had to be for Stick Insect! He stood nervously onstage as the judges whispered together.

Then Dog announced:
"**S** is for . . .

" . . . **Sloth!**"

"No!" cried Stick Insect. "Can I do T?" he begged. "A lot of people mistake me for a Twig."

But Dog announced:
"**T** is for . . . **Tapir!**"

Umbrella Bird and Unicorn lined up for the letter U.
"A unicorn is just a horse with a horn!" shouted Pony.

U went to **Umbrella Bird**.
Stick Insect comforted Unicorn.
"I'm sure you'll get into another book," he said.

The judges whizzed through **V**, **W**, **X** and **Y**.

And then there was just one letter left.
"There's no one for Z!" Dog cried.
"Pony sent Zebra away."
"A zebra's just a stripy horse,"
explained Pony.

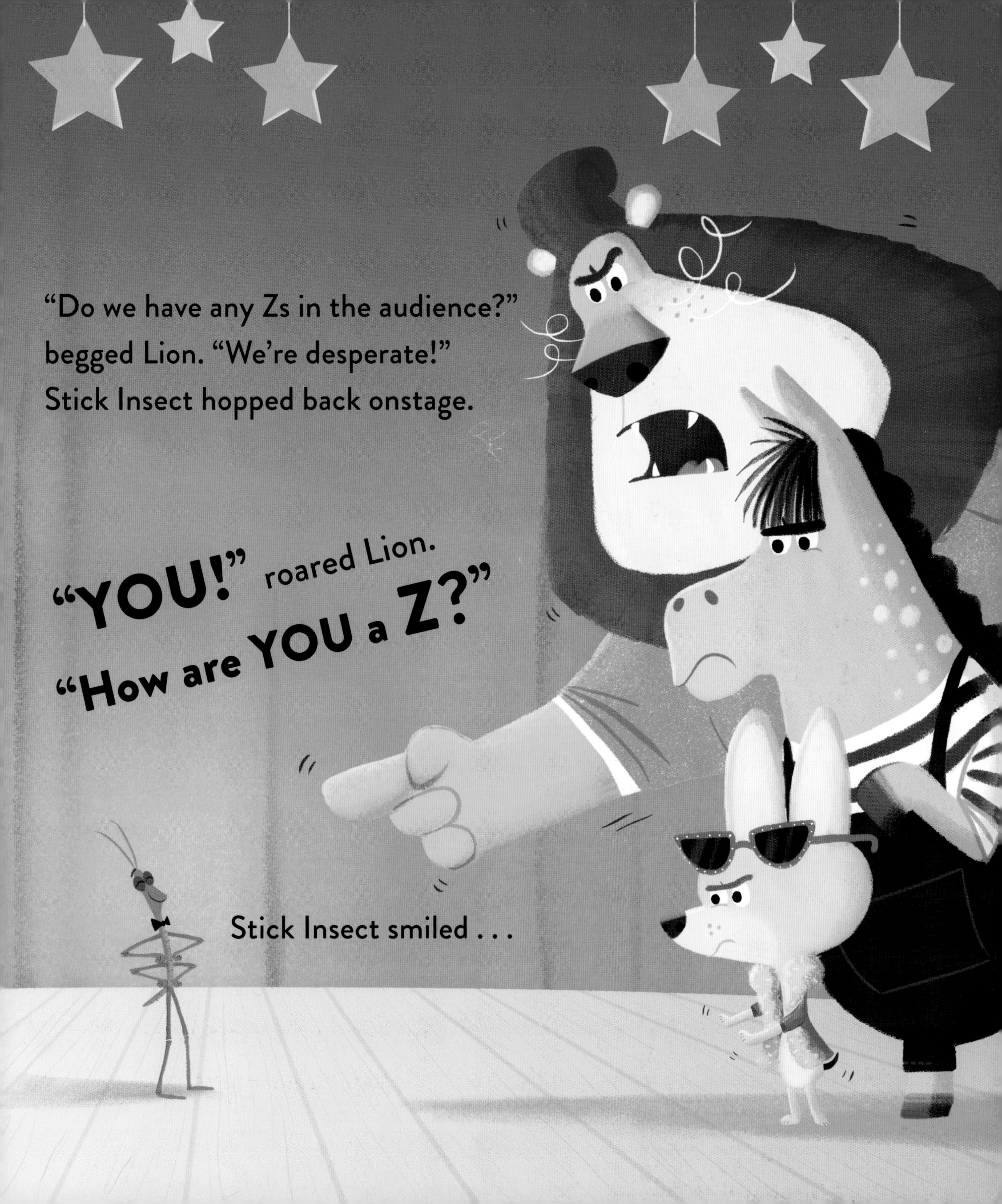

"Do we have any Zs in the audience?" begged Lion. "We're desperate!" Stick Insect hopped back onstage.

"YOU!" roared Lion.

"How are YOU a Z?"

Stick Insect smiled . . .

"My name is **Zac**."

Dog's Amazing ABC!

Illustrated by Pony

Axolotl

Brontosaurus

Capybara

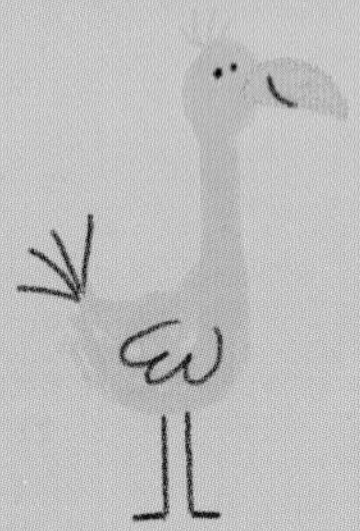

Dodo

Echidna

Flying Squirrel

Gnat

Hammerhead Shark

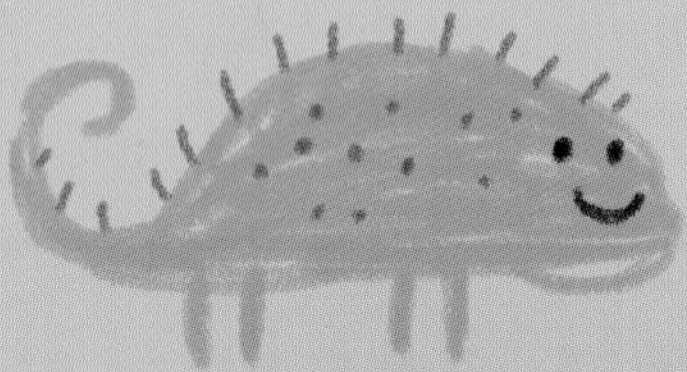

Iguana

Jackalope

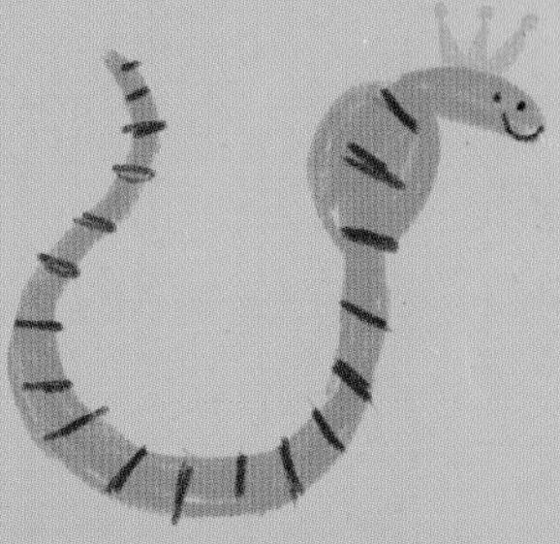

King Cobra

Lemmings

Manatee
Naked Mole Rat
(wearing clothes)
Opossum
Pangolin
Quetzal
Rockhopper Penguin
Sloth
Tapir
Umbrella Bird
Vulture
Weasel
X-Ray Fish
Yak
Zac

DOG'S AMAZING ABC